DK READERS

Power Rangers Jungle Fury

We Are the Power Rangers

Written by Amy Junor

BEGINNING
1
TO READ

DK

The Jungle Fury Power Rangers are warriors with Kung Fu skills.

They protect the Earth from an evil spirit called Dai Shi. Each Jungle Fury Power Ranger fights using the special powers of a wild animal.

Casey is the Red Ranger.
He is the leader of the Power
Rangers. Casey fights with the
power of a tiger.

Like a tiger, Casey is tough and
strong. He is also a fierce fighter.

tiger

The Red Ranger wears a special red helmet. His helmet covers his face. It protects his face in battle.

helmet

Theo Martin is
the Blue Power
Ranger.

Theo always tries to follow the rules. He likes to stay out of trouble. But he is on the same team as the rebel Casey, so it is hard to avoid trouble!

Theo fights with the power of a jaguar. Jaguars are clever, fast fighters, just like Theo.
When he is fighting, Theo moves quickly and smoothly like a jaguar.

jaguar

13

Lily Chilman is the Yellow Power Ranger. She was captain of the cheer squad at her school. She is also a tough fighter.

Lily fights with the power of the cheetah. Like a cheetah, Lily is calm in battle, with lightning-fast moves.

cheetah

Robert James
is known as RJ.
He is the Violet Power
Ranger. He is also
a Kung Fu Master.

RJ trains the other Power Rangers. He fights with the power of the wolf.

wolf

RJ first started learning Kung Fu
when he was a young boy.
He has been training all his life.

Now he has a lot to teach
the other Power Rangers!

Power Rangers ride into battle on powerful robot vehicles called zords.

tail

Casey's zord looks like a tiger with a stripy tail.

Theo's zord is in the shape of a jaguar and has sharp claws.

Jaguars are one of the fastest animals on Earth. The Blue Ranger's zord is one of the fastest vehicles.

claw

A group of Kung Fu warriors called the Order of the Claw locked the evil spirit of Dai Shi in a special box.

When Dai Shi escaped, the Power Rangers had to save the world.

The Red Ranger
called his zord to help
him battle Dai Shi.
The evil spirit
was very strong.

Casey needed the help of his zord and all the other Rangers to beat Dai Shi.

The Power Rangers combined
their zords to make a big,
powerful Megazord.

Nothing can defeat a Megazord!

The Megazord defeated
Dai Shi and
the world
was saved.

Picture word list

tiger

page 7

wolf

page 19

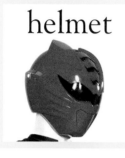
helmet

page 8

tail

page 22

jaguar

page 13

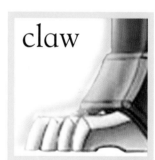
claw

page 25

cheetah

page 16